THIMBLE
HOLIDAY HAVOC

Jon Blake lives in Cardiff with his partner and two young children. He qualified as a teacher in 1979. His first story was published in 1984; since then he has earned his living as a writer of books, TV and radio scripts, and as a teacher of creative writing. Previous books include the bestselling *You're a Hero Daley B*, *Stinky Fingers' House of Fun* and *The Last Free Cat*. His first Thimble book, *Thimble Monkey Superstar* was published in 2016. It was selected for the Summer Reading Challenge and shortlisted for the Lollies 2017 Laugh out Loud Book Awards.

Martin Chatterton's own books include *Monster and Chips* (OUP) and some of the *Middle School* books with James Patterson, and he has illustrated many, many books in the UK and Australia, including stories by Julia Donaldson and Tony Bradman.

First published in 2017
by Firefly Press
25 Gabalfa Road, Llandaff North,
Cardiff, CF14 2JJ
www.fireflypress.co.uk

A CIP catalogue record of this book
is available from the British Library.

ISBN 9781910080665
ebook ISBN 9781910080672

*This book has been published with the support
of the Welsh Books Council.*

Design by: Claire Brisley
Printed and bound by: PULSIO SARL

THIMBLE
HOLIDAY HAVOC

JON BLAKE

Firefly

**ILLUSTRATED BY
MARTIN CHATTERTON**

CONTENTS

Thanks to Jordi Blake for his enthusiasm,

ideas and help with the chapter headings

PROLOGUE
THE LIST

Dad leaned back in the remains of his favourite chair and pressed the ends of his fingers together. That was the way he always sat when he was pretending to be intelligent.

'Let's go through the list one more time, Jams,' he said.

'Things Thimble must not get his hands on,' I began. 'Number one, the electric drill.'

Dad frowned. 'The drill is in the reinforced strongbox?'

'Yes, Dad,' I replied wearily. It was the fifth time he'd asked me this.

'With the double padlock?'

'With the double padlock.'

'Continue,' said Dad.

'Number two. The matches.'

Dad gave a little shudder then waved me on.

'Number three,' I said. 'The saw.'

Dad shifted uncomfortably. It was not easy to sit in a chair whose legs were six inches long.

'Number four. The microwave.'

Dad gave a weary groan.

'Dad,' I suggested, 'why don't we just put "Everything"?'

'If we do that,' replied Dad, 'he will have won.'

'OK. Number five...' I paused. 'Are you feeling strong, Dad?'

'Just get on with it.'

'The superglue,' I said.

No response.

'The superglue,' I repeated.

'Yes, I heard what you said,' hissed Dad.

'Dad, do you remember the time…'

'Next!' said Dad.

'It would make a great story,' I suggested.

Dad fixed me with his fiercest stare. 'No, Jams. It would not make a great story. It would make an extremely embarrassing and humiliating story. No one must ever know what happened when Thimble got hold of the superglue!'

CHAPTER ONE
WHAT HAPPENED WHEN THIMBLE GOT HOLD OF THE SUPERGLUE

It was a rare day in Dawson Castle, our little bungalow home. Rare because Dad was happy. As you may know, Dad is the great children's author Douglas Dawson, except not many people seem to have noticed how great he is. As a result he does not sell many books, or visit many schools, or do anything much, except moan about the fact that Mum has much more money. So you can imagine how delighted he was when a letter arrived asking him to be the guest speaker at the Lower Pugley Retired Ladies Embroidery Club annual dinner. I was a little suspicious about this, as there is a man on telly called Douglas Lawson who makes tapestries out of pasta and was voted Silver Fox of the Year. But I said nothing. How could I spoil it when Dad was marching round the house with his fist raised high, crying 'They want me! They want me!'?

As the day approached Dad grew more and more nervous. He couldn't decide whether to wear his green corduroy suit or his paisley shirt and cravat. He couldn't decide whether to get a haircut or wear his Terry Pratchett hat. He stopped eating tea and started collecting pens, always a bad sign with Dad. Then, when the day arrived, he decided that fourteen pens simply weren't enough.

'Jams,' he said. 'Where is my lucky pen?'

'In the Useful Drawer?' I suggested.

'Of course,' he replied. 'That's where it'll be.'

The Useful Drawer was in the castle refectory (kitchen), just under the Utensils We Don't Understand Drawer. We hurried there with all possible speed, only to find the drawer suspiciously open and Thimble lurking even more suspiciously nearby. To Thimble, the Useful Drawer was a place of endless fascination, perhaps because I had once unwisely hidden a banana there.

'Thimble,' asked Dad, 'have you just taken something from that drawer?'

Thimble's only answer was to back further away.

'He's got something behind his back, Dad.'

'What have you got behind your back, Thimble?' asked Dad.

Thimble let out a stream of meaningless monkey chatter.

'You're making him feel threatened, Dad.'

'He is threatened,' said Dad.

'What is it, Thimble?' I asked. 'Is it drawing pins? Is it sellotape? Is it corn-on-the-cob holders?'

'The corn-on-the-cob holders are in the cutlery drawer,' said Dad.

'Not any more, Dad. Mum moved them.'

'What in heaven's name for?'

'It was when she was de-cluttering,' I replied.

'That is not an answer,' said Dad.

The discussion had only lasted half a minute, but as we all know, you can't take your eyes off Thimble for two seconds. He was gone.

'Get the pen, Jams,' said Dad. 'I'm more nervous than ever now. You'll find me in the dungeon.'

The dungeon is Dad's name for the toilet in Dawson Castle. Mum sometimes spends half a day in there, possibly to get away from Dad, but Dad prides himself in taking as little time as possible, so it was a surprise when he did not reappear for several minutes. Anxiously I knocked on the dungeon door.

'Are you alright, Dad?'

'No, something is very wrong.'

'In what sense?' I asked.

'In the sense,' replied Dad, 'that I cannot get off the toilet.'

'Oh dear. How do you think that's happened?'

'When you looked in the Useful Drawer,' said Dad, 'did you notice if the superglue was there?'

'Come to think of it,' I said, 'it wasn't in its

usual place.'

'Bring me the phone. I need to ring your mother.'

'Do you think that's a good idea?' I asked. 'You know how Mum hates…'

'Bring me the phone NOW!' yelled Dad.

I brought Dad the phone, secretly switching on the speakerphone in case they had a row and I had to give evidence in court.

'Nora?' said Dad.

'Douglas?' said Mum.

'You have to come home this minute!' said Dad.

Mum laughed.

'I mean it. The taxi's coming in twenty minutes and I'm stuck to the toilet!'

Mum laughed louder. 'What are you stuck by?'

'Well, I'm not stuck by my face, am I?'

'I don't know,' said Mum.

'I don't eat from the toilet!'

'What's sticking you?'

'Superglue,' said Dad.

'Superglue? How did that get there?'

'Thimble got hold of it.'

Mum laughed again.

'Nora, this is no laughing matter!'

'They can get it off in A and E,' said Mum.

'A and E?' said Dad. 'How am I going to get to A and E? I'm stuck to the toilet!'

'Just take the seat off.'

'What, and walk down the road with it stuck to my backside?'

'Listen,' said Mum, 'the Abermouth wind farm is running at half power and I'm up to my eyeballs. You'll have to sort it out yourself.'

'But it's your fault!' said Dad.

'Why?' said Mum.

'You invited the monkey to live with us!'

No reply.

Mum was gone.

'Jams!' cried Dad. 'Get a spanner and a screwdriver and a crowbar and remove this seat from the toilet!'

It was actually quite easy to get the seat off the toilet as it was just fixed with two wingnuts.

But getting the seat off Dad was another matter.

'Shall I give it a yank, Dad?' I suggested.

'No way!' said Dad. 'You'll pull the skin off my

bottom!'

'But if we leave it you'll never get your trousers on.'

'Unless they're very big trousers,' said Dad.

'What about Grandad's enormous dungarees?' I suggested.

It was a stroke of genius. Dad's dad had been a gigantic man and when he died Mum kept his dungarees for me to use as a beach tent. They would easily fit over Dad and the toilet seat as well.

'But I'll look ridiculous!' said Dad.

I checked my watch. 'Fifteen minutes till taxi time,' I said.

Dad groaned. 'Fetch the dungarees,' he said.

As predicted, Grandad's enormous dungarees went on easily. You could probably have fitted the whole toilet into them. Unfortunately, however, they hung down like limp folds of skin and you could still clearly see the outline of the toilet seat.

'We need to bulk them out, Dad,' I said.

'What with?'

'Plastic bags?' I suggested.

'They'll rustle,' said Dad.

'Old socks?'

'Be very heavy,' said Dad.

'Bubble wrap?'

'We haven't got any.'

'I know!' I said. 'Balloons!'

It was another stroke of genius. But there was one problem. Blowing up twenty balloons would take me half an hour. Unless, of course, I did what I saw on YouTube: fixed them over the nozzle of a tap, and filled them with water!

It worked a treat. I didn't actually tell Dad what I'd done, in case he panicked, but the dungarees filled up nicely, and there was no danger of the balloons escaping thanks to the cycle clips I fitted round Dad's ankles.

'How do I look?' asked Dad.

'Good,' I replied. 'No sign of the toilet seat.'

'Showtime,' said Dad. He picked up his briefcase and headed for the North Gate, which is what Dad calls the front door. But just as he was passing down the hallway something caught his eye.

'What on earth is that doing there?'

There on the sideboard lay an axe – the long-handled axe Dad used for chopping firewood.

'Thimble must have been using it,' I said.

'What on earth for?' asked Dad, much

alarmed.

'He was probably just playing,' I said. 'If he'd been chopping up the furniture we'd have heard it.'

'We'd better put it somewhere he'll never find it again,' said Dad. He seized the axe in his right hand, but as he did so a new look of alarm came over his face.

'What is it, Dad?'

'Hell's bells!' cried Dad. 'More superglue!'

I went to wrench the axe from Dad's grasp but he furiously waved me away. 'Don't be an idiot, Jams!' he cried. 'You'll be stuck to it as well!'

Dad flung his arm one way then the other but there was no moving the axe.

'I can't go outside like this!' he cried. 'The neighbours will think I've gone bonkers!'

'Maybe you should wear a disguise, Dad.'

'What could I wear?' asked Dad.

I was thrown for a moment as I hadn't expected Dad to agree. But Dad was sure the taxi could still take him to A and E where both the axe and the toilet seat could be removed. He might be late for his talk but it was better late than never.

'I've got that clown mask I made at summer camp,' I suggested.

'Get it,' said Dad.

This was a proud moment for me. Dad never took much notice of things I made, and he'd certainly never worn one of them. But the clown mask fitted perfectly.

'How do I look?' asked Dad, his voice rather muffled.

'To be honest,' I replied, 'a little bit scary.'

'Never mind that,' said Dad. 'Will anyone recognise me?'

'Er ... no,' I replied.

Dad checked his watch, forgetting that

the axe was attached to his arm, and completely demolished Mum's favourite table lamp. 'Taxi's due,' he said, ignoring the devastation.

We exited Dawson Castle.

'Let's try not to attract attention,' said Dad.

'OK, Dad,' I replied. Unfortunately however, we had barely got onto the pavement when we were approached by a bull mastiff. My *Observers Book of Dogs* says that, statistically, the bull mastiff is the fifth most likely dog to bite, and this one certainly did not look like it wanted to play fetch. Its ears were back, its teeth were bared and it was emitting a low, sinister growl.

'I don't think it likes you, Dad,' I said.

'Get away!' cried Dad. 'Get away you

stupid – **YOW!**'

Yikes! The horrible hound had bitten Dad right on the dungarees! There was a loud **POP**, then suddenly a big wet patch spread across the front of them.

'There's something ... wet ... going down my leg,' gasped Dad.

I said nothing.

'Do you think it's blood?' asked Dad.

There was no time to reply. The taxi had turned into the street and was heading towards us. Just as it should have slowed down, however, the driver caught sight of Dad and started to speed up again.

'It's not going to stop,' said Dad.

'Flag him down with your axe.'

'Oy!' cried Dad, doing as I suggested, but unfortunately the taxi was already past us and Dad merely succeeded in slicing off the wing mirror. We watched helplessly as the mirror clattered into the gutter and the taxi disappeared from view.

A few neighbours appeared at their windows.

'Seen enough?' cried Dad. 'Happy now?'

'Don't make it worse, Dad,' I advised.

'Worse? How could things possibly get worse?'

Dad sank into the gutter, his clown face in his hands. At this point a police car came screaming round the corner, siren blaring. Two burly policewomen leapt from the car and demanded that Dad drop the weapon. Needless to say he did not comply, leaving them with no option but to arrest him.

CHAPTER TWO
STRANGERS IN THE CASTLE AND A BIT OF PHOTOSHOPPING

Thimble, as you might have gathered, creates a lot of havoc. But he is also my best friend. He sleeps on my bed at night and helps me on with my splints in the morning. My splints are plastic things which I wear round my calves and feet. They keep my feet flat to the ground and stop me from walking on tiptoes, which might be great for ballet but is useless for football. I have taught Thimble to play football. He is a brilliant goalie, really bendy, like Gordon Banks in his prime, except Gordon Banks never stuffed the ball down his shorts and ran off with it.

Anyway, on with the story.

It was a wild windy night at Dawson Castle. The rain lashed at the castle defences. Mum looked glum and Dad looked glummer.

'I'm sure the weather was better before that monkey came,' he said.

'Don't talk about Thimble as if he isn't here,' said Mum. 'He understands everything.'

'He can't speak,' said Dad.

'How many times must we tell you,' I replied. 'He speaks in sign language and everyone understands it except you.'

Dad turned to Thimble. 'What's the sign for "Dad"?' he asked.

Thimble blew a raspberry.

'See? He doesn't know.'

We said nothing.

Outside, the rain was getting heavier.

'What a miserable summer,' said Dad.

'We need a holiday,' said Mum.

'We can't afford it,' said Dad.

'Actually,' said Mum, 'there is a way we can afford a holiday.'

'How, Mum?' I asked.

'Just leave it to me,' said Mum.

Next day it was still raining, Dad was still glum, but Mum said she had some great news.

'Holiday's sorted,' she said.

'Brilliant!' I cried.

'Hang on,' said Dad. 'How much?'

'Not one penny,' said Mum.

'Explain,' said Dad.

'You remember that site I found on the web?'

'Not ... nestswap.com?' said Dad.

'That's the one. Remember, you said it was the height of lunacy to let total strangers stay in your house while you stay in theirs?'

'Tell me you haven't arranged a home swap!'

'It'll be fine,' said Mum.

'It will not be fine!' railed Dad. 'A man's home is his castle! You don't let total strangers into your castle!'

'This is a woman's home,' said Mum. 'I paid for it.'

'I'm paying you back!' cried Dad.

'When you write a bestseller,' replied Mum, 'i.e. never.'

'Don't say that!' said Dad.

'Where are we going, Mum? I asked.

'Blingville. Where they hold the film festival.'

'Wicked!' I said. 'Isn't that in France?'

'The south of France. Guaranteed sunshine.'

'At least that rules out Thimble coming,' grunted Dad.

'Why?' I replied.

'I can hardly see us getting a monkey through customs,' said Dad.

Mum said nothing.

'Nora. You're not thinking of smuggling Thimble through customs, are you?'

'We can't leave him here,' said Mum.

'Of course we can! We'll put him in kennels or something!'

'Monkey kennels?' I said.

'Or something,' said Dad.

'He's coming,' said Mum, 'and that's that.'

'And how exactly do you propose getting a monkey past passport control?' asked Dad.

'You remember my friend in the passport office?'

'What, the crook?' said Dad.

'She's not a crook,' protested Mum. 'She just believes in the free movement of people. And monkeys.'

'You'll never get her to…'

Mum laid a passport on the table. Dad seized it. 'Timothy Dawson?' he cried. 'Timothy Dawson? Hang on, what about the photo…? Hell's bells, what did you do to him?'

'Just a wig and some face paint,' said
Mum. 'Then a bit of photoshopping.'

Dad was aghast. 'Why did you give him
my surname?' he protested.

'You're always saying you're the head of
the household,' said Mum.

'Head of the human household!' said
Dad. 'Not the monkey one!'

'What about his tail, Mum?' I asked.

'We'll roll that up and stick it in his trousers,' said Mum. 'It'll just look like he's got a big bum.'

'I need to think about this,' said Dad.

'Think quickly,' said Mum. 'We leave tomorrow.'

CHAPTER THREE

A FAST MOUSTACHE AND A SUSPICIOUS DARK THING ON THE SOFA

Everything was going fine till we reached Passport Control. There were two booths in front of us, each manned by a stern-looking border guard. Thimble went right, I went left. The guard checked my passport, then my face, then showed the passport to a machine.

At this point I had a strange sensation. Something was tickling the side of my face. I raised my hand and grasped something woolly.

Yikes! Thimble's tail! It must have broken free of his trousers!

There was no time to lose. Quick as a

flash, I bent the tail over my top lip and tried to look as innocent as possible.

The guard's eyes rose. A look of confusion came to his face. He checked the passport, then me, then the passport again.

'You didn't have that moustache a minute ago,' he said.

'It grows fast,' I blabbed.

'You're not old enough to grow a moustache!' he replied.

'Run, Thimble!' I cried.

In a trice the moustache had vanished from my face and I was following Thimble helter-skelter through the departure lounge. Sirens were going off all around us and men with guns were appearing everywhere.

'Mum!' I cried.

A distant voice replied, 'Yes, love?'

'Where are you, Mum?' I cried.

'Right here,' said Mum, 'with your milk.'

Sure enough, there was dear Mother, wearing her dressing gown, holding my even dearer morning milk.

'Had a bad dream, Mum,' I said.

'Never mind,' said Mum. 'You're back in real life now. Come and help me shave Thimble's face.'

Two hours later, the keys to Dawson Castle
were under the flowerpot, and we were
on our way to 33, Rue de Fou, Blingville.
I knew the address because it was my job
to remember it, which was easy, as 44 was
Mum's age, and it was exactly eleven years
less. It was hard to contain my excitement,
and even harder to contain Thimble's. He
could not get used to having no tail and
every few minutes did a sudden about
turn in hope of taking it by surprise. Sadly,
however, his tail was too smart for him,
especially with ten strips of gaffer tape
sealing it to his underpants.

Everything was going fine till we reached
Passport Control. There were two booths in
front of us, each manned by a stern-looking
border guard. I went right and Thimble
was about to go left when Mum swung him

round in front of me.

'Let's all go through together,' she said.

The border guard took Thimble's passport, stared hard at it, then at Thimble. Then the passport again, then Thimble again. She frowned hard, as if dealing with some insurmountable problem.

'We're in luck,' said Mum. 'Prosopagnosia.'

'Wow,' I said, 'what's that?'

'Face blindness.'

'Face blindness?' I repeated. 'What's she doing working in passport control?'

'Nepotism,' said Mum.

'How do you know?' I asked.

'I'm omniscient,' said Mum.

I'll leave a little break here so you can check a Glossary of Long Difficult Words. Mum has a degree in English Literature and likes to talk to me as if I have one too.

It was late and quite dark when we arrived in Blingville. You could tell we were in France because everyone was speaking French, even the taxi drivers. As usual in these situations, Dad took control. Dad was proud of his command of the French language. For some strange reason, however, the taxi drivers refused to understand a word he said and turned to Thimble instead, whose sign language is international. So it was Thimble who booked us a taxi, me who showed them the address scribbled in my notebook, and Mum who sat in the front chatting and, for some strange reason, being understood perfectly well.

Yes, everything was looking ticketyboo, especially when we arrived at 33, Rue de Fou and found a magnificent villa with a front garden bigger than the whole of Dawson Castle. Grapes were cascading over the front wall and, just as Serge and Colette had promised, there was a grey wheelie bin alongside the front door.

'The keys should be taped inside the lid,' said Mum.

Dad checked. 'No keys here,' he grunted.

'Perhaps they've fallen inside?' suggested Mum.

Dad checked inside increasingly frantically, finally turning the bin upside down and shaking it like a tambourine.

'I knew this home swap was a mistake!' he cried.

'That is strange,' said Mum. 'Serge and Colette did not seem like the kind of people who would forget to leave the keys.'

'We don't even know them!' railed Dad.

'We've exchanged emails.'

'That's all we are going to exchange,' said Dad.

'Maybe there's a way in round the back,' said Mum.

We made our way down the drive, which seemed to go on forever, till we reached the back of the house. There we found a terrace with a huge outdoor table and fancy curly chairs. Beyond that was a garden of scorched grass in which there was a gigantic trampoline, a colossal swimming pool and a mammoth tree house. It was a garden beyond my wildest dreams.

'Maybe we could just live here,' I suggested.

Dad did not seem to hear me. He was rattling the shutters that covered the French windows and checking if there was any way to climb up to the first-floor balcony.

'Wow,' said Mum. 'This really is swish. I hope they're not disappointed with our bungalow.'

'At least they can get into our bungalow!' replied Dad.

'Hang on,' said Mum. 'There's an open window.'

I followed Mum's pointy finger. Yes, there was an open window, at the very end of the house. But it was a very small window, probably the window to a toilet.

'We can't get through there,' said Dad.

'Thimble could,' said Mum.

I called Thimble, who by now was dangling from the tree house.

'Thimble,' I said, 'listen very carefully. We want you to climb through that window, then open one of those big windows and let us in. Do you understand?'

Thimble nodded enthusiastically.

'He understands.'

'He nods whatever we say,' said Dad.

Thimble nodded enthusiastically.

'Heaven help us,' said Dad.

I gave Thimble a leg up, not that he needed it, and he scrambled through the window with the greatest of ease. A few seconds passed. Then a few more. Then a few minutes. Then a few minutes more.

'Perhaps there aren't any keys,' I suggested.

'This kind of window is usually locked with a handle,' said Mum.

'If we could just get … these … shutters…' grunted Dad, heaving with all his might at the great wooden window guards.

'Try lifting the catch,' said Mum. She raised a metal catch and hey presto, the shutters folded back and we had our first glimpse of the interior of 33, Rue de Fou.

Wow. It really was plush. Chandeliers, marble floor, antique dressers and a luxurious pure white sofa on which sat Thimble, a slice of cake in his hand, watching telly.

'Thimble!' cried Dad. 'Put that down and let us in!'

Thimble waved, let out a stream of monkey chatter, then went back to watching telly.

'This is a disaster!' cried Dad. 'Can you imagine the havoc he'll create if he's left alone in there?'

'Thimble,' said Mum, 'be a good monkey and open this window.'

As usual, Thimble was more inclined to listen to Mum. He got off the sofa, came towards us and began examining the window. Then, just as it seemed our wait was over, something distracted his attention and he disappeared from view.

'Lord give me patience,' said Dad, which seemed unlikely.

At this point I spotted something.

Something very suspicious.

'What's that on the sofa?' I asked.

'Where?' asked Mum.

'Where Thimble was sitting.'.

'The dark thing?' asked Mum.

'Hell's bells!' I cried. 'It's a poo!'

Next thing I knew, Dad had seized one of the garden chairs.

'Move aside, Jams,' he commanded.

'Dad!' I cried. 'You're not going to...'

KER-RASSSSH!

Either the chair was very strong, or the window very weak, but all that was left was a metal frame with a few shards of glass hanging. The rest of the glass was spread randomly over the pristine marble floor, while the chair had gone on to demolish a coffee table and the vase which had been on it, spilling dirty green water over a pile of nearby books. Thimble could be heard gibbering frantically in the nearby kitchen, while Mum simply stood with her head in her hands.

'I never realised you were so strong, Dad,' I said.

Dad did not reply. He was in a kind of trance, panting heavily. I made my way carefully through the devastation and inspected the dark object on the sofa.

'Would you believe it?' I said. 'It's a TV remote.'

CHAPTER FOUR
THIMBLE'S IDEA OF HEAVEN AND RED MEANS STOP

The glazier did his best with the window next morning, but it totally didn't match the others, and when he handed the bill to Mum her face dropped.

'So much for the free holiday,' she said.

'I told you not to bring Thimble,' said Dad.

'Thimble didn't break the window,' said Mum.

'Or the vase,' I added helpfully.

'This place is chock full of valuables,' said Dad. 'It's going to be a nightmare keeping Thimble away from them.'

'Maybe we should make another list,' I suggested.

'Good idea,' said Dad.

I opened my notebook and wrote:

THINGS THIMBLE MUST NOT GET
HIS HANDS ON IN THE HOLIDAY
HOME.

We progressed round the house, noting the ornaments, the tablecloths, the rugs, the stereos, the lamps, the lead crystal wine glasses and the framed photographs. There was one wall which was covered in pictures of speedboats, except on closer inspection it turned out to be just one boat, *Le Superb*. The boat sure lived up to its name.

'Do you think that's their boat?' I asked.

'Who cares,' said Dad.

'Maybe we could go on it!'

'It's a house swap,' said Dad. 'Not a boat swap.'

'Just imagine though!' I said.

'What, Thimble getting his hands on it?'
said Dad. 'I'd rather not.'

We moved on. There was one door
we hadn't tried yet, a locked door in the
kitchen. The door was painted bright red,
which I thought might be a warning, but
no, it was just an enormous garage, full
of tellies and stereos and enough tinned
food to keep an army. There was also a
workbench on which we found a saw, a box
of matches, an electric drill and a tube of
superglue.

'Wow!' I said. 'This would be Thimble's
idea of heaven!'

Dad picked up the superglue and winced.
'Thimble,' he said, 'must never get into this
room.'

'What's that under the bench?' I asked.
I could see the edge of a large chest, like a

pirate's treasure chest.

'I think we've seen enough.'

'Let's just look inside, Dad!' I replied.

'No, let's go,' said Dad. 'This place is making me nervous.'

Dad locked the red door, checked the locked door three times, then placed the key under a tray of cutlery in a kitchen drawer. Just as he closed the drawer, however, he became aware that someone, besides me, was watching him.

'Thimble!' he cried. 'What are you doing here?'

It was a rather stupid question. As usual, Thimble wanted to join in with whatever we were doing, which always looked like some kind of game to him.

'It's OK, Dad,' I said. 'He doesn't know what the key is for.'

'Don't mention the key!' said Dad.

'He probably saw it,' I replied. 'Did you see the key, Thimble?'

Thimble nodded eagerly.

'And did you see Dad lock the garage with it?'

'Don't say that!' said Dad.

Thimble looked from Dad to me and back again several times. This was starting to look like a particularly good game.

Dad gave a great sigh. 'Well done, Jams!' he said, retrieving the key. 'Now you can find somewhere to hide it!'

I took the key and set off. Thimble bounded after me.

'Not you, Thimble!' cried Dad.

'Distract him, Dad,' I said.

Dad mimed hitting himself in the face with a cricket bat. This may not mean much to you if you have not read *Thimble Monkey Superstar*, but it meant an awful lot to Thimble, who could not relive this memory often enough.

I took my chance and hurried upstairs. I was immediately drawn to the room with the photos of *Le Superb*. There was an antique desk in this room with a set of drawers above it, higher than Thimble could reach. I opened the first drawer, only to find another set of keys already there. Beneath these was a book: *Le Superb: Manuel D'instruction*.

If only I could read French!

I flicked through the pages. Hang on a minute … could this maybe be the superboat's *instruction manual*? And this being the case, could that set of keys be the *keys to the boat*?

'Dad!' I cried, racing downstairs.

'Ssh,' said Dad. 'I'm teaching Thimble something.'

'But Dad,' I said. 'I've found...'

'RED MEANS STOP', said Dad. 'Do you understand, Thimble?' Dad pointed at the red door.

'I'm not sure if that's a good idea, Dad', I said.

'Just like a RED TRAFFIC LIGHT.' continued Dad. 'RED MEANS STOP. Now show you understand.'

Thimble did the hand signals for Red Means Stop.

'Does he understand?' said Dad.

'Yes, Dad,' I said, 'but don't forget he always does the opposite of everything you say.'

'We'll see,' said Dad. 'Now what on earth is your mother doing?'

I glanced through the window to see Mum standing on a chair, trying to look over the garden fence. Thinking I might get more sense out of her than Dad, I went outside with the boat keys.

'What are you doing, Mum?' I asked.

'Trying to see the neighbours.'

'Why?' I asked.

'Because, unlike your dad,' said Mum, 'I like to meet people. And besides, what if there's an emergency?'

'We'll be alright,' I said.

'They're not there anyway,' said Mum. 'No signs of life at all. We'll just have to be very careful not to do anything risky.'

'Right, Mum,' I replied. 'Guess what, Mum – they've got a speedboat, and I've just found the keys!'

CHAPTER FIVE
IN WHICH NOTHING IS GOING TO HAPPEN, EXCEPT IT DOES

Mum was most surprised to find out about the speedboat. Serge and Colette had never mentioned a boat.

'But, Mum,' I said. 'You said they said we were welcome to use anything we found.'

'I think they were talking about saucepans,' said Mum.

'Oh, Mum, please!' I pleaded.

'I want to have a relaxing time on this holiday,' said Mum. 'That means lying on the beach sunning myself, not worrying about you and Thimble. You know nothing about boats and nor do I.'

'What's the worst that could happen?' I asked.

'Nothing is going to happen', said Mum, 'because we are all going to the beach.'

I groaned. 'Can't we just look at the boat? Look, it says on the keys, C492. That must be where it's parked.'

'Berthed', said Mum.

'See?' I said. 'You do know about boats.'

I put on my most appealing face and kissed Mum all over her hand. She weakened. 'I don't suppose there's any harm in looking at it', she said.

It was as if she had fired a starting pistol. I was dressed for the beach in five minutes flat. I even helped Thimble on with his bathers and applied my own sun cream. Dad didn't put on sun cream because he said it was just an excuse for chemists to make money out of us.

'Douglas,' said Mum, 'this is the South of France. It's very hot out there.'

'I'll keep my corduroy suit on,' said Dad, 'And my Terry Pratchett hat.'

'You'll fry!' said Mum. 'Haven't you brought any shorts?'

'I don't have any shorts,' said Dad.

'Well, make some. Cut down some of your trousers.'

'What a ridiculous idea,' said Dad.

'Maybe I'll find a nice French man to take me to the beach,' said Mum. 'They dress so well.'

'I dress well!' protested Dad.

'They dress so well in shorts,' said Mum.

'Oh, for heaven's sake,' said Dad. 'Where are the scissors?'

Thimble was listening to this conversation

with great interest, but when Dad appeared
in his cut-off trousers it must have scared
him because he promptly disappeared. To

be fair, it was quite scary.

'Wow, Dad,' I said. 'Your legs are so white! Have they ever been in the sun?'

'Sun ages the skin,' grunted Dad.

'You'd better put on some sun cream,' said Mum.

'Nonsense. Now, will they do or won't they?'

Mum studied Dad closely. 'Oh, Douglas,' she said, 'there's a big stain down the front.'

'I know,' said Dad. 'That's where Thimble spilt the printing ink all over me.'

'You can't go out like that,' said Mum.

'I'm a writer!' protested Dad. 'I can go out like anything!'

'Not with me you can't,' said Mum. 'Go and make another pair.'

'I'll have no trousers left,' moaned Dad. He trudged back up the stairs, muttering and spluttering – but suddenly the mutters and splutters were replaced by an almighty cry. 'Thimble! You ... monkey devil!'

I hurried up the stairs to find a scene of utter chaos. Dad's trousers were spread all over his bed – or I should say, the remains of Dad's trousers. Every pair had the legs cut off. Not at the knee or halfway up the thigh, but right at the top, higher than a pair of boxer shorts.

'Dad! You shouldn't have left the scissors out.'

'Typical!' railed Dad. 'Blame me, not the monkey!'

'He's got an instinct to cut,' I said.

'Well, I've got an instinct to...'

Dad stopped short as Mum entered the room. 'Oh, Thimble, you are naughty,' she said. 'But at least Dad's got lots of shorts now.'

'And no trousers,' said Dad.

'Let's see what they look like,' said Mum.

Teeth grit hard, Dad pulled on the nearest
pair of cut-offs. Mum tittered and Thimble
gave a little whoop.

'Wow, Dad,' I said. 'They look like hot
pants.'

'I can't wear these!' cried Dad.

'But, Dad,' I said. 'You said you were a

writer, so you could wear anything.'

'Wear a long t-shirt,' suggested Mum.

Dad put on his longest t-shirt.

'Now it looks like you're wearing a mini-dress,' I said.

'And pregnant,' added Mum, helpfully. Dad does have a bit of a beer belly.

'Good,' said Dad. 'I'm glad I've given you a laugh. Fortunately I still have my Terry Pratchett hat. People will take me seriously as long as I'm wearing that.'

Luckily there were lots of people in Blingville with shorts as short as Dad's. Mind you, most of these were women, and most of these women had a little dog sitting on their hand, not a monkey trailing behind them. We did get a few funny looks when we reached the beach, but this may have been because of Thimble. There was a shower on the beach and this interested Thimble greatly. Several times he lolloped towards it, only to be called back by Mum. We tried to explain that it was a people shower, not a monkey shower, but to Thimble it was just a lovely little waterfall.

It wasn't long before I started to get bored, and so did Dad. We couldn't see the point of just lying in the sun like Mum.

'I want to see the boat,' I moaned.

'I'll tell you what,' said Mum. 'Why don't just you and your dad go and look at the boat, so I can have some peace?'

'What about Thimble?'

'I don't think it's a good idea if Thimble goes near the boat,' said Mum.

'Why? We're not going on it.'

'Very well,' said Mum. 'But you must

promise to keep Thimble well away.'

'I swear,' I said, 'on my mother's life.'

'Let's make it your father's,' said Mum.

Thimble, Dad and I made our way round the harbour. There sure were a lot of boats, huge, shiny expensive ones. But nothing compared to the boat at berth number C492.

'Wow,' I said, 'that is awesome.'

'Flashy, I call it,' said Dad.

Awesome and flashy. Yes, that did describe the monstrous vessel before us. Serge and Colette must have robbed a bank to buy it.

'Wouldn't it be great to have just one little tour round the harbour?' I said.

'Control yourself, Jams,' said Dad.

At this point I became aware that we were being watched by a group of teenagers. I

am used to people looking at me because
I use a walker and walk a bit different.
But these teenagers were not interested
in me. They were interested in Dad, or
more particularly, his shorts, which were
obviously a style they had never seen
before. They pointed, called out a few
things in French, then laughed loudly, also
in French.

Dad's blood began to boil. 'Don't they
know who I am?' he grunted.

'Maybe they can't read,' I replied,
humouring him.

The teenagers were not getting any less
interested. Some of them were pulling up
their own shorts and sticking out their
bellies. Then one of them said something
about Dad's Terry Pratchett hat.

That was the final straw for Dad. 'Get on

the boat, Jams,' he ordered.

'Wha…' I began.

'Just get on the boat!' hissed Dad.

Dad grabbed my walker, and with a bit of help from Thimble I clambered onto *Le Superb*. Thimble and Dad followed.

The teenagers were now silent.

'What's the matter, kids?' cried Dad. 'Haven't you got a boat? No, because you're a bunch of nobodies, not the world's greatest author. Start her up, Jams!'

'Eh? I said.

'You've got the keys!' cried Dad. 'Start her up!'

'If you say so, Dad,' I replied. I turned the key in the ignition and there was a powerful THRUM.

'Now,' said Dad, 'what's the form here?'

Dad studied the controls, and after a

few moments of trying to look intelligent, engaged the engine. The boat set off, backwards, and almost immediately came to a sudden violent stop.

'Did we hit something?' I asked.

'Maybe the engine stalled,' said Dad.

'Engine's still going, Dad.'

I looked around and saw we were still tied to the jetty.

'Shouldn't you have untied those ropes, Dad?' I said.

'It's called casting off,' grunted Dad, as if knowing the right words made him look less stupid.

We cast off, forgetting the engine was still in gear. As a result the boat leapt backwards like a rodeo bull. There was a loud CRUNCH.

'Now we *have* hit something,' I said.

'Good,' said Dad. He really was in a bad mood, possibly because the teenagers were laughing harder than ever. Dad's answer to this was to set the speed to max and leave them in a trail of spray. Soon they were no more than specks in the distance and we were halfway across the bay, looking like world champion speedboaters, apart from the fact that we were still going backwards.

Maybe Thimble sensed we needed help. Two small hairy hands came up alongside Dad's and attempted to take control of the steering.

'Oh no, you don't,' said Dad. 'Jams, take Thimble down into the hold.'

I didn't actually know what the hold was, and I suspect Dad didn't either, but there were steps going below deck and I duly took Thimble down them. We found a bedroom there, a very plush one, full of interesting-looking cupboards which would no doubt keep Thimble amused for hours. I ordered him to remain there and hurried back to help Dad, who by now was halfway across the harbour, still going backwards. By now lots of other boats were taking a keen interest in us. Hooters were going off all over the place.

'What do you think that means, Dad?' I asked.

'Must be some kind of salute,' replied Dad.

'Do you think they recognise you?'

'Possible,' said Dad.

'Dad...' I began.

'Yes?' said Dad.

'Can we stop now?'

'Aren't you enjoying it?' asked Dad.

'I think I'd enjoy it more,' I replied, 'if we were going forwards.'

'I like to do things differently,' said Dad.

There was another BANG.

'What was that?' I asked.

'Just a buoy,' said Dad.

'A boy?' I repeated. 'Dad, I really think we should stop!'

Reluctantly, Dad stopped the boat, and just to be sure it wouldn't start again, switched off the engine. Which was strange, because there was still a steady BRRRRR sound.

'Why is the engine still making a noise?' I asked.

'Is that the engine?' said Dad.

'What else could it be?' I asked.

Suddenly a look of alarm came over Dad. 'Thimble!' he cried.

Nothing could have prepared us for the sight which greeted us below deck. Thimble was standing in the corner of the bedroom, having a lovely shower, except there had been no shower the last time I'd been there. With mounting horror I spotted an open cupboard, a cordless electric drill and a row of neat holes in the boat's hull, through which came the refreshing jets of water Thimble was so enjoying.

'No-o-o-o-o-o!' I cried.

'Plug them up!' cried Dad.

I looked around in desperation and saw a small fridge. Inside was a pack of sausages. With fumbling fingers I broke the sausages apart and stuffed the squishy meat into the holes. But the strength of the water was too great, and I ended up having my own shower of sausage blobs.

'It's hopeless, Dad,' I cried. By now the
bedroom was a foot deep in water.

'Abandon ship!' cried Dad. Dad was easily
panicked, and Thimble was quick to pick
up on the atmosphere of fear. We scrabbled
up on deck, located the boat's dinghy and,
after an age of panicky kerfuffling, got it
onto the water, along with my walker and

the three of us. Dad laid back panting with his hand on his heart while Thimble and I took an oar each. Meanwhile *Le Superb* began to list heavily and by the time we reached shore had become a new adventure playground for the crabs.

'Could things get any worse?' said Dad, flopping onto a harbourside bench.

'Oh look,' I replied. 'Here comes Mum.'

Mum was sauntering up towards us, a broad smile on her face. She gave me a kiss, Thimble a hug, and Dad a pat on the back.

'For the first time in ages,' she said, 'I actually feel relaxed.'

'That's good, Mum,' I replied.

'There's nothing better,' she said, 'than to lie back with the sun on your face and forget about all your cares. Now, where's this boat?'

'Er,' I began.

'C492, wasn't that the number?' said Mum.

'We've moved it,' said Dad.

The trace of a frown came back to Mum's face. 'Moved it?' she repeated. 'Where?'

'Out there,' said Dad, with a vague sweep of his arm.

Mum stared out into the great expanse of the bay. 'Where out there?'

'Oh,' said Dad, 'round about the middle.'

Mum looked again. 'I can't see a boat in the middle.'

'No,' said Dad, 'it's in the, er...'

'Underground car park,' I babbled.

Mum's frown deepened. 'Underground car park?' she repeated.

'No, what's that thing that boats have?' I blabbed. 'Underwater boat park.'

Dad put a hand to his head. Mum's face, by now, was back to its normal expression.

'Are you telling me,' she said, 'that you have sunk Serge and Colette's boat?'

'No,' said Dad, suddenly defiant, 'we have not sunk anything.' He pointed a shaky finger at Thimble. 'That thing has.'

'Don't blame Thimble,' said Mum. 'You're the responsible adult.'

'Yes, I am a responsible adult,' said Dad, 'which is why I didn't want to take in that monkey in the first place! If there's anyone to blame for the boat sinking, it's you!'

'Don't be childish,' said Mum.

'Oh, childish am I?' railed Dad. He folded his arms and stamped his foot. 'Well, maybe you should just find yourself another boyfriend!'

'Maybe I should,' muttered Mum.

CHAPTER SIX
A LARGE FLOCK OF BUTTERFLIES AND A WOUNDED ELEPHANT

'So, Jams,' said Dad. 'We've worked out the cost of the boat, and we've worked out how much I earn a year. Now all we have to do is to work out how many years it will take me to afford a new one.'

I tapped the numbers into the calculator on Mum's phone. 'Hmm,' I said.

'Well?'

'Nine hundred and fifty-seven years, Dad.'

'Are you sure?'

'Trust me.'

'It's the phone I don't trust,' said Dad.

'Let's face it, Dad,' I said, 'we'll never be able to buy them a new boat.'

Dad frowned deeply. 'The trouble with me,' he said, 'is that I'm too honest.'

'How do you mean, Dad?' I replied.

'Well,' said Dad, 'a dishonest person would just stage a burglary and tell Serge and Paulette the burglars took the boat keys.'

'Tell Serge and *Colette* the burglars took the boat keys,' I said.

Dad looked shocked. 'What are you suggesting, Jams?' he said.

'It's what you said, Dad!' I protested.

'OK,' said Dad. 'We'll do it. But remember it was your idea.'

Before we go any further, I would like to put it on record that it was not my idea to burgle the house we were living in, and nor was it my idea to dress Thimble as a burglar. For a start I have no idea how burglars dress. Dad does, but I think this may have come from the comics he read when he was six. Frankly Thimble looked ridiculous in a hooped t-shirt and bandit mask, but at least the bag on his back didn't have SWAG written across it.

'Mum isn't going to like this.'

'Mum's not here,' Dad grunted.

'Where is she?'

'According to the note she left,' replied Dad, 'she's down the butcher's again.'

'She's been three times since yesterday,' I said. 'That seems a lot of times, especially for a vegetarian.'

'I don't like the way that butcher winks at her,' growled Dad.

'She says he's got a tic,' I replied.

'Oh yes?' said Dad. 'Well, how come he

doesn't have this tic when he looks at me?'

'Thimble's getting impatient, Dad,' I said, changing the subject.

Dad focussed on Thimble, who knew something important was expected of him, and was anxious to find out what.

'Thimble,' said Dad, 'we need you to be a burglar. Do you understand what a burglar is?'

Thimble nodded eagerly.

'He doesn't, Dad,' I said.

'A burglar,' said Dad, 'is someone who goes somewhere they're not supposed to go.'

Thimble's interest grew.

'A burglar,' said Dad, 'is someone who goes into a house which is not their house, and takes things they shouldn't take. Do you understand?'

Thimble nodded eagerly.

'Does he?' asked Dad.

'I think so this time,' I replied.

'Good,' said Dad. 'Now we're all going to go outside the house, and I am going to make a video of you being a burglar. Just be natural, and don't smile for the camera.'

We exited the front door and I gave Dad Mum's phone.

'What's that for?' said Dad.

'Shooting the video,' I replied.

'I thought that was a calculator,' said Dad.

'Maybe I should do it,' I replied, retrieving the phone. 'All set, Thimble?'

Thimble nodded in the usual way.

'On your marks … get set … GO!'

Thimble shot off round the side of the house.

'Where's he going?' said Dad.

'Must be going round the back,' I replied.

We hurried after Thimble, just in time to see him scaling the garden fence.

'No, Thimble!' I cried. 'This house! Not the neighbours!'

Dad stamped his foot. 'What is wrong with that monkey?'

'It was your instructions, Dad,' I replied. 'You shouldn't have said he had to go into a

house which wasn't his house.'

'This house isn't his house!' stormed Dad.

'Thimble doesn't know that,' I replied. 'As far as he is concerned, this is where we live now.'

'We'll be living in jail if we don't get him out of there!' said Dad. He fetched a small stepladder and climbed up to look over the fence.

'Where is he, Dad?'

'Inside.'

'Wow, that's clever,' I said. 'What's he doing?'

'Sitting on the sofa,' replied Dad, 'eating a slice of cake.'

'You did tell him to take things he shouldn't take.'

'For Pete's sake!' said Dad. 'What's he going to take next?'

There was a creak. We looked anxiously at next door's gate, only to realise it was ours that was open. Mum had come home.

'What are you doing up there, Douglas?' she asked.

'That's my business,' said Dad.

'Did you have a nice time at the butchers?' I asked, changing the subject.

'Yes,' said Mum. 'We had a very interesting chat.'

'I bet,' said Dad.

'About the neighbours,' added Mum.

'Have you found out all about them, Mum?'

'Yes. I should get down from that fence, if I were you, Douglas.'

'Why?' said Dad.

'They're criminals,' replied Mum. 'Dangerous criminals.'

A large flock of butterflies took off in my stomach. 'Are you sure?'

'Oh yes,' said Mum. 'They are called the Viborgs. They rob jewellery stores.'

'Then why aren't they in jail?' I asked.

'They've bribed the chief of police,' replied Mum.

'Bribed the chief of police? Then why doesn't the mayor sack the chief of police?'

'They've bribed the mayor as well.'

'Wow,' I said, 'these Viborgs sound like real big shots.'

'Real big shots,' replied Mum, 'with real big shotguns.'

Dad lowered his head below the top of the fence.

'Where's Thimble?' asked Mum.

'Hmm,' I replied. 'Where is Thimble, Dad?'

Dad shrugged.

'Why are you on that stepladder?' asked Mum.

Dad shrugged again.

'Let me get up on there,' said Mum.

Dad seized the top of the stepladder and held on hard.

'Douglas,' said Mum, 'you're being ridiculously childish.'

Dad held on even harder. Mum's eyes narrowed. 'Is Thimble next door?' she asked.

'It was Dad's idea!' I blurted.

'It was Jams' idea!' blurted Dad.

A big fat tear welled up in my eye. 'Can you get him back, Mum?' I pleaded.

Mum thought for a moment. 'Is there a drill anywhere?' she asked.

'No way!' said Dad.

'It's in the garage, Mum,' I said.

If you've ever waved a piece of liver under a cat's nose you will be able to picture Thimble when he saw the drill. His concentration on it was total. Out he came, as if hypnotised, all the way to the fence, which was where he seemed to smell a rat.

'Here, Thimble,' I prompted. 'Here, Thimmy-thimmy-thimmy-thimmy-thimble!'

Very cautiously, Thimble began to climb the fence. I almost had him when he saw Dad's face and changed his mind.

'Come on, Thimble,' I said. 'Nice electric drill to play with.'

A great battle was going on in Thimble's mind but neither side was winning.

I tried another tack. 'Listen, Thimble, you've got to get out of there! A bad man lives there!

'Bad man, Thimble. Do you understand? Bad man.'

Thimble pointed at Dad.

'No, Thimble,' I said. 'Dad's not a bad man! Well, sometimes maybe, but not bad like this man! This man is a criminal, Thimble – someone who takes things which don't belong to him.'

Thimble pointed at Dad.

'No, Thimble, Dad's not a criminal. OK, I know he took the boat, and told you to burgle the house…'

'He did what?' said Mum.

'There was a good reason for it,' said Dad. 'Trust me.'

Mum gave Dad a look which suggested she would rather trust a scorpion.

'Thimble,' I said, 'We

absolutely promise that if you come over here, you can play with this lovely drill.'

Thimble looked at Mum, who nodded. At last he climbed over the fence, landed at my feet and gave my splints a hug.

'Put the drill back in the garage, Jams,' said Dad.

'Douglas, you can't do that,' said Mum.

'Why not?' said Dad.

'Because he'll never trust us again.'

'I know,' I suggested. 'How about if we tell him he can just drill one hole? He can't do much harm drilling one hole.'

'That seems like a good idea,' said Mum.

'Crazy,' said Dad.

I explained the rule to Thimble, who, as usual, nodded eagerly. Mum went off to put some pork chops in the fridge and I duly handed the drill to Thimble. He lolloped off with it, as happy as a sand monkey, and I put my hands over my eyes.

'Why are you covering your eyes?' asked Dad.

'It's because the sun's so bright,' I replied.

A few seconds later, I heard a distinct BRRRRRRR.

'What's happening?' I asked.

'I don't know,' replied Dad.

'Why not?'

'Because I'm covering my eyes too.'

The BRRRRRRR stopped. Thimble had been as good as his word. When I finally plucked up courage to open my eyes, there was no sign of him, or the drill.

It was then I had a strange sensation.

'Why are my feet wet, Dad?'

'I don't know,' replied Dad. 'Have you weed yourself?'

'Don't think so,' I replied. 'It's not warm.'

'Wait a minute,' said Dad. 'My feet are wet too.'

'Have you weed yourself, Dad?'

'Don't be ridiculous.'

'Maybe it's rain,' I said.

'It hasn't rained since we arrived,' said Dad.

'So where's the water coming from?'

We cast our eyes around for the solution.

'No-o-o-o-o-o-o-o!' I cried.

'The swimming pool!' cried Dad.

There was nothing we could do. The lovely blue pool was crumpling like a wounded elephant, water streaming from its side. Soon there was no water inside, and nothing but a heap of blue plastic where the pool used to be.

'Let's look at the positives,' said Dad.

'Yes,' I agreed, 'there's always positives.'

'The lawn needed watering,' said Dad.

The pool took up loads of space,' I said.

'Most importantly,' said Dad, 'it's your mother's fault.'

'Let's go and tell her now,' I suggested.

'Wait,' said Dad. 'We still don't know where Thimble is.'

'Or the drill,' I added.

We hurried into the house, only to realise that the garage was still open. By some miracle, however, Thimble was sitting outside the red door, still holding the drill.

'Good boy, Thimble!' I said. 'Apart from destroying the swimming pool, which you must never do again, not that you'll get the chance.'

'See?' said Dad, suddenly cheering up. 'I've trained him. Red means stop!'

Sure enough, Thimble made the hands sign for Red Means Stop.

'Well done, Dad,' I said. 'I was sure that you teaching Thimble that would lead to disaster.'

Somehow, however, I guessed that this was not the end of the story. Thimble looked far from happy when we took the drill from him, and made the saddest sound imaginable when we went into the garage without him. He knew it was a place of heavenly promise now. And I have to admit I glanced back more than once at that tempting treasure chest of who-knows-what poking out from beneath the workbench.

CHAPTER SEVEN
WARNING - MAY CONTAIN TRACES OF A NUT CALLED DAD

Mum was not keen to take the blame for the ruin of the pool. It was Dad's fault Thimble had burgled the neighbours, and Dad's fault Thimble hadn't been supervised properly.

Dad begged to differ. That's what you call it when someone argues back. Dad argued back a lot, begging to differ in a louder and louder voice, till Mum said, 'DOUGLAS I'VE HAD ENOUGH I AM DETERMINED TO ENJOY THIS HOLIDAY AND IF I CAN'T ENJOY IT WITH YOU I SHALL ENJOY IT WITHOUT YOU.'

A few minutes later Dad arrived in my room looking very red in the face.

'Jams, get your shoes on,' he said. 'I'm going to have a fight and I need a witness.'

'Not with Mum?'

'No, not with Mum...'

'Who then?' I asked.

'The butcher.'

'What?'

Dad sat on the edge of the bed and huffed out a few big breaths. 'Your mother,' he said, 'is abandoning us.'

'Never,' I said.

'There's a do on tonight,' said Dad. 'Some kind of ridiculous music and fireworks thing. The butcher's going to be there, and Nora's going to...'

'What?'

'...see him,' said Dad.

'That's bad.'

'Except she won't be seeing him,' said Dad, 'because I am going to see him first!' Dad stood up to his full height and pounded his fist into his palm.

'Dad,' I said, 'do you think it would be a good idea to get some trousers first? He might not take you seriously in hot pants.'

'He'll take me seriously enough when I knock his block off,' said Dad.

'Wow. That sounds violent, Dad.'

'I feel violent,' said Dad.

Dad was certainly talking a good fight, but I was relieved when he decided that Thimble should come too. The butcher would think twice before tangling with a monkey.

'Can I get some bus fare off Mum?' I asked. 'It's a long way to the butcher's.'

Dad gave a tired sigh.

'It's ok, Dad,' I said. 'I won't say we're going to beat up her new boyfriend. I'll say we're going to the fair to play hook-a-duck.'

Fortunately Mum suspected nothing and we set off on our quest without incident. The sun shone, a few birds twittered, and the world seemed quite unaware that World War Three was about to start.

'What's French for "butcher"?' I asked.

'*Boucher*,' replied Dad.

'Hey, everyone!' I cried. '*Mon papa* is going to have a fight *avec le boucher!*'

'Zip it, Jams!' hissed Dad.

'I can't help it! I'm excited! I've never seen you have a fight before! I bet you'll marmalise him, Dad!'

Dad did not reply. He was starting to look a bit green around the gills.

'Are you alright, Dad?'

'Of course I'm not alright!' snapped Dad.

'You'll marmalise him!' I repeated.

'Jams, just shut up about this fight!'

My natural optimism was beginning to fade. I did not sense that Dad was relishing the confrontation. As the butcher's shop came into view, he became very stiff in his movements and started muttering under his breath.

'Tis a far far better thing I do,' he said, 'than I have ever done.'

'Wow, Dad,' I replied. 'That's like poetry.'

'*Tale of Two Cities*,' said Dad. 'Charles Dickens.'

'Oh,' I replied, 'I thought you'd written it.'

'I might have written it,' said Dad, 'if he hadn't written it first.'

We reached the shop. It was only now

that we realised how many people were inside it.

'Oh,' said Dad. 'There's a queue.'

'What are you going to do, Dad?' I asked.

'We can't just barge in,' said Dad. 'We're British.'

We joined the queue.

'Seems a bit weird,' I said, 'queuing up to have a fight.'

Dad said nothing. His eyes were fixed on *le boucher*. The butcher was a tall man, with a mop of dark curls tied back in a ponytail, deep brown eyes and cheekbones like Elvis. He smiled readily at his customers as he doled out their treats with forearms like Popeye.

'Look at those muscles, Dad,' I said. 'Do you think he works out?'

Dad could not resist a glance at his own

spindly limbs, which never worked out on anything but a keyboard.

'Gyms,' he noted, 'are for the vain and ignorant.'

Slowly the queue moved forward. Every customer departed happy, to a booming *au revoir* from the butcher.

'He's very popular, Dad.'

'As long as the till's ringing,' grunted Dad.

'Yeah, as long as the till's ringing,' I repeated, not quite sure what this meant. 'Do you know what, Dad? I really hate him.'

There was a little growl from Thimble. He also understood that the big tall man was the enemy. But just then, the big tall man spotted him. His eyes lit up.

'*Un singe!*' he said. '*Un petit singe!*'

Everyone turned to us.

'What did he say?' I asked.

'How do I know?' snapped Dad.

Hell's bells! The butcher was coming out from behind the counter!

'What are you going to do, Dad?' I asked.

Dad swallowed hard.

'Slap him round the face with your glove, Dad,' I said, 'and challenge him to a duel!'

'Jams, will you shut up!' hissed Dad.

Entirely ignoring us, the butcher grabbed Thimble and hoisted him onto his shoulder.

'*Bonjour, mon petit!*' he said, with a wink.

'Did you see that? He winked at Thimble! Maybe it is a tic, Dad. He can't fancy Thimble.'

'*Qu-est-ce-que tu veux, mon petit?*' asked the butcher.

'He doesn't speak French,' I said.

'Ah!' said the butcher. 'I am so sorree! What would you like, my little one? I do

not have the bananas!'

Everyone laughed. To my dismay, Thimble had been completely won over and now rested his head on the butcher's shoulder.

'Do something, Dad!' I cried. 'Now he's got Thimble as well!'

Dad did not respond. The butcher turned

to me. 'And this must be your master!' he said. 'A good-looking master for a good-looking monkey! What is your name, big man?'

'Jams,' I muttered.

'Jams!' repeated the butcher. 'And what can I do for you today, Jams?'

'Dad?' I said.

For a moment the whole of time seemed to stop. Then, without warning, Dad's hand shot out. Before the butcher knew what had hit him, Dad had grabbed a string of sausages and legged it. 'That's for winking at my partner!' he cried, just before he disappeared from view.

No one seemed to understand what had just happened.

'Er ... how much do we owe you?' I asked, opening Mum's purse.

With a baffled shake of the head, the butcher lowered Thimble to the ground and fished in the purse for a few coins. Thimble gazed into the space Dad had occupied and made some sign language.

'That's right, Thimble,' I said. 'Bad man.'

CHAPTER EIGHT
RED MEANS GO AND DAD FINALLY PUNCHES SOMETHING

We found Dad halfway home, slumped on a bench with the sausages hanging round his neck. He looked gloomy.

'What happened, Dad?'

'Too many people.'

'I paid for the sausages,' I said.

'What sausages?'

'The ones hanging round your neck.'

Dad glanced down, removed the porky necklace and draped it over a nearby bush. 'You should have given him Thimble instead,' he said.

I covered Thimble's ears. 'Why d'you say that?'

'He obviously preferred the butcher to me,' said Dad.

'You should try being nicer to him.'

'Now you sound like Nora,' said Dad. A hand came up to his head. The thought of Mum had made him even gloomier.

'What are we going to do?' I asked.

Dad shrugged.

'It'll be awful if she goes off with the butcher,' I said. 'Well, not awful, because he'll probably take us swimming which you don't do, and I expect he's got a car which you haven't, and obviously he's nicer to Thimble...'

'Jams,' said Dad.

'Yes, Dad?'

'Do us a favour,' said Dad, 'and stop talking.'

I stopped talking.

But not for long.

'You might still beat him in a fight,' I said, 'if you got a gang together, say with the criminals next door…'

'Jams!' snapped Dad. 'It's not going to happen!'

'But, Dad!' I protested. 'She's still going to see him tonight! We've got to do something!'

'What do you suggest?' said Dad.

I thought for a moment, which is how long it takes for the first thing to come into my head. 'We should follow her, Dad,' I said. 'Like private eyes! Then if it looks like she's going to kiss him, we'll send Thimble in to break it up!'

The thought of Mum kissing the butcher was enough to make Dad surrender all common sense and take me seriously.

'What if she sees us?' he asked.

'She won't see us. We'll be very careful.'

'OK,' said Dad. 'But remember, this was your idea.'

Night had fallen when Mum finally set off. In Blingville that meant bright lights and lots of hustle and bustle. Hustle and bustle always made Thimble excitable, so it was going to be hard to keep control of him. We explained that we were playing a game, a bit like Grandma's Footsteps, where we had to tiptoe very softly and stop dead if Mum turned round. Thimble was very good at this at first, but as we got closer to town, I could sense him starting to get edgy. Town really was very crowded, cars bumper-to-bumper, people shoulder-to-shoulder, dogs nose-to-tail and mosquitoes cheek-by-jowl.

'Does it have to be this busy?' said Dad, who didn't much like cars, or people, or dogs, or mosquitoes.

'It must be because of the fireworks,' I said, but just then I noticed a big crowd of paparazzi at the movie theatre, with an even bigger crowd of people penned behind them. A plush limo was arriving and the excitement was intense.

'Hold steady now, Thimble,' I warned.

The limo doors opened. Holy Moly! It was only Salman Carr and Louella Parker, the most famous film star couple in the world!

'It's Salmanella!' I cried, using the name by which they were known in the celeb mags.

'Means nothing to me,' said Dad.

'I've got to get their autographs, Dad!' I cried.

My enthusiasm was fatal. The moment I

started running, Thimble raced on ahead
of me, having obviously decided he needed
their autographs as well. Being a small and
tricky monkey, he managed to slip right
through the crowd, past the paparazzi,
the bodyguards and the barriers, right on
to the red carpet which was waiting for
Salmanella.

At this point he looked down, and
immediately froze.

'Get that monkey out of the way!'
someone cried.

Thimble was going nowhere. Salmanella's
bodyguard moved towards him, but as
soon as Thimble sensed a threat, his natural
instinct kicked in and he went bonkers,
baring his teeth and letting loose a fearful
stream of high-pitched gibberish. That
scared the bodyguard, but not half as much

as it scared Salmanella, who leapt back
into their limo and commanded the driver
to get them the bejasus out of there. The
limo went off in a screech of tyres and in a
few seconds had disappeared, to a howl of
dismay from the crowd.

'Sorry, everyone,' I said, working
my walker through to the front and

immediately being surrounded by paparazzi. 'It was Dad's fault.'

'Uh?' came the reply. '*La faute de papa*?'

'*Oui*', I said. '*La faute de papa!*' I turned to Thimble. 'Dad got it wrong, Thimble,' I said. 'Red means stop in Britain, but go in France! Understand, Thimble? RED MEANS GO!'

Thimble looked down at the carpet, then back at me, several times.

'RED MEANS GO, Thimble!' I repeated. 'Go, now, quickly!'

Thimble took my hand and lolloped obediently off the carpet.

'Good boy, Thimble,' I said. 'Now, never listen to Dad again. Have I said sorry, everybody? What's sorry in French?'

'*Desolé*,' said the bodyguard.

'Pleased to meet you, Des,' I replied. 'Jams

Cogan. Now Thimble, where's Mum?'

'Lost,' came the reply. Dad had arrived.

'*C'est papa!*' someone shouted. There was a chorus of deafening boos.

'You'd better get out of here, Dad,' I said, 'before you get lynched.'

'What have I done?' protested Dad. The only answer was even louder boos, so Dad wisely chose to leave the scene of disaster as quickly as possible. But which way were we to go now? There was no sign of Mum anywhere.

'Let's try the night market,' I suggested. 'Mum likes shopping in the dark.'

The night market stretched down the side of the harbour. There were stalls selling everything from baby clothes to baby cheeses. A mass of colourful lights hung above the stalls, and above that a starless night awaited the firework display. We might have really enjoyed the atmosphere if we were not gripped by panic.

'She must be somewhere,' said Dad.

'Everybody is somewhere,' I replied.

'Do you have anything useful to say?' asked Dad.

'Yes,' I replied. 'There's a bandstand down there. We're probably in the right place for the music.'

Dad shuddered. He didn't like music, unless it was written five hundred years ago and played by gloomy-looking people in suits. Thimble, on the other hand, loved just about any music, and knew exactly what I was talking about. He took the lead, getting faster and faster, while Dad and I puffed and panted in his wake. As the bandstand approached, however, he stopped. Something had caught his eye.

'What is it, Thimble?' I asked, but his only reply was to shoot off for the bandstand like ten devils were after him.

'Maybe he's seen Mum,' I said.

But it was not Mum that Thimble had seen. Up on the bandstand, a band was getting ready to play, and chatting to them was none other than our greatest enemy – well, Dad's greatest enemy – *le boucher*!

Thimble and the butcher greeted each other like long-lost friends. The butcher gave Thimble a bear hug, a fireman's lift and an aeroplane spin. Thimble showered the butcher with kisses and beat on his head like a bongo drum.

'Dad!' I said. 'Do something!'

Dad seemed unable to do anything.

'Right!' I said. 'I will!'

I ditched my walker and went up to the bandstand. But it was a big step up, and no matter how hard I tried, I couldn't get my foot that high. Watching me struggle must have finally stirred Dad into action, because next thing I knew, his hand was on my shoulder.

'OK, Jams,' he said. 'Leave it to me.'

Dad leapt up onto the bandstand, but as he did so there was an enormous RIPPPP as the seam at the back of his hot pants gave way. Lesser men might have retreated, but Dad marched on, one arm outstretched towards Thimble, the other holding the back of his shorts together.

'Excuse me, old boy!' he cried. 'That is my…'

No one got to hear the word monkey. That was because the air had suddenly been filled by deafening rock music. The band had kicked off, Thimble was back on the floor, and the butcher was releasing his ponytail and shaking out a massive mane of curly hair. Next second, the microphone was in his hands.

Who'd have believed it? The popular, likeable, well-built, good-looking butcher was also a rock star!

Thimble, not surprisingly, was now going bananas. I had taught Thimble many dances, from head-shoulders-knees-and-toes to the macarena, and Thimble was now trying the whole lot out, in random order, to whoops and hollers from the crowd.

Dad, however, was determined to put a stop to this. He did his best to grab Thimble, but Thimble was too fast for him and he wound up clutching thin air. When

Dad did finally lay a hand on Thimble there was a massive boo from the crowd, and possibly because of his bad experience at the movie theatre, Dad suddenly changed tack and made out the whole thing was a funny act. He deliberately missed Thimble a couple more times, which got a laugh, possibly the worst thing that could have happened as it inspired Dad to do something even more stupid, something so stupid I had to cover my eyes.

'Please, Dad,' I muttered, 'not that.'

Fearfully, I opened my fingers a crack. No, it was not a bad dream. Dad had fallen in step with Thimble and was lamely attempting to copy his dance moves.

The crowd was laughing a lot now. Dad obviously did not know whether they were laughing with him or at him, and maybe he didn't care. His dancing got more and more extreme, until even Thimble started to hide his face in his hands. Having no new moves to copy, Dad turned his attention to the butcher.

Like a true pro, the butcher had ignored all the goings-on and was striding about the stage shaking his mighty mane. Dad watched for a few seconds, then gave his own head a little shake, causing his comb-over to flop limply from one side to the other.

'Just get off the stage, Dad,' I

muttered, but it was not to be. Dad was now hell-bent on showing the butcher that anything he could do, Dad could do better.

The butcher kicked a leg in the air. Dad kicked a leg in the air.

The butcher punched the air with a fist. Dad punched the air with a fist.

The butcher leapt like a gazelle and came down in the splits.

Dad leapt like a gazelle and…

AAAAAAAAAAAAAARGHHHH!

Dad's cry of pain did not need a microphone. I can't easily describe how he had landed, other than to say it was not how the butcher had landed, and certainly not better than the butcher had landed. The best word I can think of for Dad's landing is WRONG.

At this point I felt a hand on my shoulder.

'Mum. Thank God you're here! Quick, phone for an ambulance!'

'The ambulance is on its way,' replied Mum. 'I rang as soon as your dad started dancing.'

CHAPTER NINE

A DISAPPEARING SAUSAGE AND THIMBLE'S TREASURE TROVE

It was a lovely hospital, the one in Blingville. I sat on a bed chatting to Dad while Thimble busily gobbled all Dad's grapes and Mum rang the travel insurance people to check if we were covered for destroying a window, a vase, a swimming pool, a luxury boat and the bottom half of Dad's body.

'So how is the, er ... what was it you hurt?' I asked.

'Let's not talk about it,' Dad replied.

'At least we got Mum away from the butcher.'

'None of this would have happened,' said

Dad, 'if Nora had explained she was just going to see him play.'

'He was very good though,' I said.

'It wasn't proper music,' said Dad, by which he meant music from five hundred years ago played by gloomy people in suits.

I didn't bother to argue. Dad was in need of support, and not just from that contraption above the bed.

'Maybe you should give Mum a special evening out.'

'How can I do that?' replied Dad. 'My back is toast! Besides, I can't leave you and Thimble in the house on your own.'

'A special evening in then,' I suggested.

'Sounds expensive.'

'Oh come on, Dad!' I said. 'You're Douglas Dawson, the great author! You can find a way!'

My words clearly struck a chord.

'You're right, Jams. No matter what ill fortune I suffer, I must never lose my self-respect. Now have a look in Mum's purse and see if she's left any change.'

'She's taken it with her, Dad.'

Dad sank back into the pillow.

'What about the sausages?' I suggested.

'What sausages?'

'The ones you left hanging on a bush,' I said. 'They might make a good meal, in a red wine sauce.'

'They've been there over a day!' replied Dad. 'If the dogs haven't had them, the sun will have turned them rotten!'

'It might improve them,' I said, 'like sun-dried tomatoes.'

'Some hope,' said Dad.

'OK,' I replied. 'We'll give one to Thimble

and if he's not sick we'll save this holiday by cooking Mum the best meal of her life!'

Luckily the dogs hadn't had the sausages. They were still hanging on the bush, exactly as Dad had left them, except they were no longer smooth and pink, but black and knobbly.

'Is it my imagination, Thimble,' I asked, 'or are they moving?'

Thimble approached the sausages cautiously and tested one with a finger. As he did so a huge swarm of flies rose into the air, and hey presto, the sausages were pink again.

'Oh, that's alright then!' I said. 'Get 'em down, Thimbs.'

Thimble lifted the sausages off the bush and handed them to me. I gave them a sniff. 'Hmm,' I said. 'Did they smell that strong before?'

Thimble shrugged.

'They do make sausages differently over here.'

Thimble nodded eagerly.

'Let's take 'em home,' I said, and take them home we did. Mum wasn't to know, of course, so we waited till she went to pick Dad up from the hospital then took out the frying pan.

'Now, Thimble,' I said, 'I am going to cook just one sausage as a special treat for you.'

Thimble looked a little doubtful, but I pressed on with the plan. I have to point out that Thimble, being a wild animal, has a very good instinct for what is edible. Many times I have found him rooting through the bins for food, quite often scoffing things

which looked utterly foul, yet no harm has
ever come of this. So there was no danger
I could poison Thimble, even though there
was a faint green tinge to the pink sausage
which grew steadily greener as it cooked.
The smell got rather stronger as well,
and I must admit I was holding my nose
as I handed a small plate containing the
delicacy to Thimble.

'A little ketchup?' I suggested. 'Or you might try mayonnaise. The French prefer mayonnaise.'

I'd hardly finished the sentence when the entire sausage disappeared into Thimble's mouth. Cooking the thing had made me feel sick enough, and the sight of it bulging from Thimble's cheek just about did for me. I rushed into the toilet and thought very seriously about retching into the sink, but luckily the feeling passed. When I returned to the kitchen there was no sign of the sausage, just one happy and healthy monkey.

'Excellent,' I said. 'Now let's look at the rest of Dad's list.'

We did so:

- Red wine sauce
- Candles

- Flowers
- Gentle music
- Other romantic stuff

'OK, Thimble,' I said. 'You go into the garden and gather some flowers. I'll find some wine.'

I knew I was taking a risk sending Thimble into the garden, but the wine was in the garage, and since I'd taught Thimble that Red Means Go, I didn't want to risk him going anywhere near the red door.

There was a whole rack of wine in the garage, so you might think it would be difficult to choose one. However, Dad had said that any old wine would do, so I simply checked the labels to see which one was oldest. That turned out to be Chateau Posheau 1954. Well, if no one had bothered to drink it since 1954, they surely wouldn't mind if we used it for sausage sauce. I dusted it off and was about to transport it to the kitchen when my eyes once again fell on the enticing treasure chest peeking out from beneath the workbench.

My heart began to thump. At last my chance to unearth its hidden secrets! I checked the window to make sure Thimble was still busy in the garden, then grabbed the chest and gave it a yank. Whatever was in there was very heavy! It took all my strength to edge the chest bit by bit into the open.

Now for the lid. It was sealed by two weighty straps, like giant trouser belts. Again it was no easy task to move the things, but my arms are strong from all the years of lugging my walker about. At last they came apart, and I was able to prise open the heavy wooden lid, to reveal ... what, exactly?

At first I thought I had luckily chanced upon a stash of candles, except they were taped together in bunches, with just one long string coming from the middle stick. I'd seen pictures of sticks like this somewhere. Maybe in a comic? With a bad guy setting light to the long string?

Yikes! That's what they were! DYNAMITE!

I quickly closed the lid, but at the last second remembered not to bang it down, because dynamite is VERY UNSTABLE, and LIKELY TO BLOW YOU TO KINGDOM COME AT ANY SECOND.

What on earth were Serge and Colette doing with it in their garage? Had the dangerous criminals next door maybe threatened them? Were they planning a bank job to become dangerous criminals themselves? My imagination was running wild, or should I say, even wilder than usual.

But there was no time to think. Thimble was on his way back from the garden, and I had to head him off before he reached the red door.

'Found some wine, Thimble!' I said. 'Oh, what's that you've got there?'

Thimble proudly laid his own treasure trove onto the kitchen table.

'Ok, let's see. Grapes … figs … almonds … tomatoes … oranges. Well, Thimble, this would make a very good Show and Tell table for a Mediterranean food project. But if you remember, the key word I uttered before sending you to the garden was flowers.'

Thimble looked gutted.

'It's all right, Thimble,' I said. 'We'll put it all in the red wine sauce.'

Thimble beamed happily. Dad's romantic meal was certainly going to be something special.

CHAPTER TEN

IN WHICH WE SAY GOODBYE TO THE HOLIDAY HOME, THAT'S FOR SURE

I didn't tell Dad about the dynamite in the garage. It wouldn't have got him in the right mood for his romantic evening with Mum. I didn't tell Mum either, because she didn't seem fantastically keen on this romantic evening, and I didn't want to give her any excuse to flee the house.

To be fair to Mum, once she saw us putting out the candles, she did agree to get dressed up. Dad was still hobbling around in his hospital pyjamas, till I persuaded him to look through Serge's wardrobe for something a bit more impressive.

Wow. That Serge certainly had expensive

taste in clothes. Everything had a designer label, even the shoelaces. I pulled out a pure white suit by Emporio Milani and held it up to Dad.

'Cool!' I said. 'You'd look wicked in this, Dad!'

'I have no desire to look anything of the sort,' said Dad, but as he held the suit in front of his Zimmer frame a little light seemed to come on in his head.

'I've seen a photo of the great author Mark Twain wearing a suit this colour,' he said.

'He's not likely to come by, is he? It wouldn't look good if you were wearing the same thing.'

'Hardly likely,' said Dad. 'He died over a hundred years ago.' He began to laugh, and even though I didn't find it the least bit funny, I joined in. Dad laughed louder, so I laughed louder, then Dad laughed louder still, so I laughed louder still, until it started getting a bit scary, at which point, thankfully, Dad threw his Zimmer frame aside and cried, 'Damn it! I will wear it!'

Everything was perfect as Dad prepared to make his entrance. The living room was festooned with candles, and I really do mean festooned, because Mum had just taught me the word and I knew exactly what it meant. The Gypsy Kings seeped from the hi-fi, a bunch of roses (picked by me) decorated the dining table, while grapes, figs, almonds, tomatoes and oranges (picked by Thimble) bubbled away in the sausage sauce on the cooker.

With due ceremony, Dad descended the

stairs into Mum's line of vision.

'Oh,' she said. 'You look different, Douglas.'

'It's the new me,' said Dad.

'Very smart.'

'You're worth it,' said Dad.

'Do you think it's a good idea to wear Serge's suit?'

'Don't spoil it, darling,' said Dad.

'It's just that … so many things have gone wrong on this holiday,' said Mum.

'Oh ye of little faith!' cried Dad. 'Nothing will go wrong tonight!'

'Hmm,' said Mum, 'just make sure you wear a napkin.'

I gave a thumbs up to Thimble. 'It's going well, Thimbs,' I said.

Thimble did not nod eagerly.

'What's the matter, Thimbs?' I asked.

Thimble gave his head a little shake and withdrew his chin into his neck.

'You're not jealous, are you, Thimbs?' I said.

Clearly I had hit the nail on the head. Thimble was so used to getting all the attention from Mum, while Dad was ignored, that this little romantic meal was a new experience to him. Ah well, I thought. He would have to get used to it. We had a meal to deliver.

And what a meal it was! Sausages in red wine sauce. … oven chips … more oven chips … and not forgetting, a few more oven chips! Mum's eyes were bulging as Thimble and I brought out the trays of food. Thimble obviously thought it looked appetising as well, since he drew up a third chair, sat himself on it, and tucked a napkin into his shirt.

'Just Thimble's idea of a joke,' I said, dragging him back into the kitchen. But Thimble was not laughing as Dad made a little joke of his own and Mum patted his hand. They really were getting on! Mum once told me of a time when she quite liked Dad, before he became all bitter and twisted, so maybe the romantic meal had brought those days back.

'It's making me hungry watching them eat,' I said.

Thimble dug into his pocket and produced a sausage.

'Wha – where did that come from?' I asked.

Thimble pointed at me.

'I never gave you that sausage,' I said. 'You ate the sausage I gave you.'

Thimble grinned.

'Thimble,' I said, 'you did eat the sausage I gave you, didn't you?'

Thimble's grin widened.

'I saw it in your mouth!' I said.

Thimble mimed spitting something out.

'Oh no,' I said. 'But you were the guinea pig!'

Anyone who has read *Thimble, Monkey Superstar*, in which Thimble was accused of being a hamster, will understand how confusing Thimble found this. But I was more concerned about Mum and Dad. They hadn't dropped dead yet, but according to my favourite book, *1001 Gruesome Diseases*, some forms of food poisoning took weeks to develop.

I suppose I could have said something as we took out the sweet course, but the evening was going so well, and besides, I had to stop Thimble trying to make a threesome again. I practically had to carry him back to the kitchen, and as Mum and Dad started spoon-feeding each other ice cream, he was literally green with jealousy.

Well, not *literally* green, because that would mean he had gone like the Incredible Hulk and actually was green, which would be quite a scary thought.

Luckily Thimble seemed to calm down when Mum went off to the toilet, so I took the opportunity to search the cupboards for the coffee cups, but turning my back on Thimble proved to be a grave mistake. When I looked round he was back in the dining room, right behind Dad, though Dad was nodding his head to the Gypsy Kings and didn't seem to be aware of this.

Tentatively, Thimble put a hand on Dad's shoulder.

'That's nice, darling,' said Dad.

Should I say something, I wondered?

Dad put his own hand over Thimble's and gently stroked his fingers.

'I've been thinking,' he said.

I really should say something, I thought.

'We've been together a long time,' said Dad.

I'll just listen a little longer, I thought, then I'll say something.

'I think it's about time,' said Dad, 'to put a ring on that finger.'

At this point Mum reappeared from the toilet. After a moment of complete befuddlement, Dad's head turned, slowly and fearfully, in search of who or what he had been petting.

'Hell's bells!' he cried. 'Thimble!' Dad's hand shot back like a bolt, smashing a glass of wine all over the front of his perfect white suit. He leapt up, not realising he had tucked the tablecloth into his collar instead of the napkin, and brought the whole

contents of the dinner table crashing to
the floor. Then he rushed to the toilet, past
a gobsmacked Mum, and started swilling
great handfuls of liquid soap and water into
his mouth.

'What on earth are you doing?' asked
Mum.

'Got to clean my mouth!' garbled Dad. 'I've just proposed to a monkey!'

Mum laughed heartily. 'Did he accept?' she said.

'It's not a laughing matter!' cried Dad.

'Oh, Douglas,' said Mum, 'stop being so pompous.'

Dad stamped his foot. 'I am not being pompous!'

'Now you're being childish,' said Mum.

'Am not!' said Dad.

'You really are,' said Mum.

Dad clamped his hands over his ears. 'La, la, la! Can't hear you!'

'Come on then, Thimble,' said Mum. 'I'll have the coffee course with you.'

'Will not!' said Dad. He snatched the candle from the table, then stormed round the room, uprooting all the other candles before throwing the lot in the waste bin.

'I'm afraid your dad's had too much wine,' said Mum.

'I have not had too much wine!' snapped Dad. 'I've had too much of THAT MONKEY!'

With those words Dad pulled on his coat and marched out into the night, slamming the door so hard the dining-room clock fell from the wall and smashed into pieces.

'Not more damage,' said Mum.

Thimble picked up the biggest remaining bit of clock and offered it hopefully to her.

'Thank you, Thimble,' said Mum.

'Do you still want coffee, Mum?' I asked.

Mum gave a deep sigh. 'No, we'd better go after him,' she said.

'What about Thimble?' I asked.

'Perhaps Thimble could tidy up,'

suggested Mum.

'Can you do that, Thimble?' I asked.

Thimble nodded eagerly.

'Let's go,' I said.

We found Dad a few hundred metres down the road. He was gazing into someone's garden.

'Look at that,' he said. 'Gnomes. I never knew the French had gnomes.'

'That's the internet for you,' I replied.

'Reminds me of the house I grew up in,' said Dad.

'That's nice.'

'From the outside, maybe,' said Dad.

'Uh-oh,' I whispered to Mum. 'He's going off on one again.'

'Isn't it strange,' said Dad, 'how enticing and homely houses look, from the outside.'

'Which reminds me,' I said. 'We'd better be getting back. Thimble will be getting anxious.'

'You've left Thimble on his own?' said Dad, suddenly snapping out of his dream world.

'Relax, Dad,' I replied. 'Everything that could go wrong on this holiday has already happened.'

'With any luck,' said Mum, 'Thimble will have tidied up by now, so we can go back and finish our lovely meal.'

'Just us?' asked Dad. 'No monkey?'

'Just us, Douglas,' said Mum.

Mum offered her elbow and Dad dutifully linked into it. We wandered back up the road, feeling pleasantly calm. As we approached the house, we could see Thimble through the window, busily preparing the room for Dad's return.

'Oh, isn't that sweet?' said Mum. 'He's put out candles again.'

'Candles?' replied Dad. 'But there were no more candles.'

'Look,' said Mum. 'The room's full of them.'

I looked. Every table, dresser, sideboard and shelf was decorated. Big, reddy-brown candles. Big, reddy-brown candles, gathered into bunches of seven, with one long wick to each bunch.

Yikes!

THOSE WEREN'T CANDLES!

'NO-0-0-0-0-0-0-0-0-0-0-0-0-0!' I cried.

I can run pretty fast when I need to, and at this moment I sure did need to. My hope was that Thimble had not lit any of the fuses, but sadly Thimble saw my arrival as the signal to do just that. He looked on in delight as the fuse fizzed like a sparkler.

'Blow it out, Thimble!' I cried.

Thimble grinned amiably, thinking this was a little joke.

'Forget it, Thimble!' I cried. 'RUN!'

I grabbed Thimble's arm and legged it, arriving panic-stricken in the garden and encouraging Mum and Dad also to run at their earliest convenience. Fortunately they were convinced by the cold sweat on my face and together we fled the garden and threw ourselves flat to the ground. There was the most almighty KER-BOOM, followed by what sounded like a hundred more KER-BOOMS, and finally the sound of tinkling glass and falling masonry. When at last all was quiet I plucked up the courage to view what was left of 33, Rue de Fou, only to

discover that the answer, basically, was a pile of rubble.

Mum and Dad appeared alongside me. Mum had a look of extreme weariness while Dad didn't really have any expression at all. He picked up two pieces of drainpipe and half-heartedly tried to fit them together.

'Let's look at the positives,' I suggested.

'Positives?' mumbled Dad.

'Yes,' I said, brightly. 'For example, we're still alive.'

'That's true,' said Dad, 'even though life is no longer worth living.'

'Maybe we could rebuild it.'

'Life?' said Dad.

'The house,' I replied. 'Well, maybe not the whole house, but at least a bit of it. Like ... a shed! Yes, that's it, a shed! Somewhere for them to come in out of the rain.'

'It hardly ever rains here,' said Dad.

'That's true,' I replied. 'Maybe they don't need a shed. Or even a house.'

Mum's phone made a noise. 'I've had a text,' she said. 'From Serge and Colette.'

Mum read the text. 'They've broken a mug,' she said. 'They want to know if they should replace it or just leave the money.'

'I hope it's not World's Best Dad,' said Dad.

'Maybe you could text them back,' I suggested, 'and break to them gently what's happened.'

'And how do you suggest I do that?' said Mum.

'You could say, that we've got some good news and some bad news. Er … what could be the good news?'

'We've had a lovely holiday?' suggested Mum.

'That's it,' I replied. 'The good news is, we've had a lovely holiday in your house. But the bad news is, we won't be having another one … because there is no house.'

Mum and Dad did not look impressed.

'I know,' I said. 'We'll get Thimble to break it to them. It won't seem so bad coming from a monkey. What's "we've blown your home to kingdom come" in sign language?'

'Jams,' said Mum, 'be quiet. People are coming.'

It was true. Folk were emerging from every house on Rue de Fou. Something like a lynch mob was heading towards us.

'We'll just tell them the monkey did it,' said Dad.

'No!' I cried. 'They'll skin him alive!'

'Better than skinning us alive,' said Dad.

I seized Thimble and hid him behind my back. 'I'll protect you, Thimbs,' I said.

The mob arrived at the gates. As they stood and stared, Dad's fear was replaced by annoyance.

'Seen enough?' he cried. 'Why don't you take a picture?'

Clearly most of the neighbours could speak English, because they immediately took out their mobiles and began snapping away.

'Did you do this?' asked a red-faced woman.

'It was the monkey,' replied Dad.

'The monkey!' cried the English-speaking people.

'*Le singe!*' cried the others.

'He didn't mean it!' I cried. 'He found

this dynamite, and thought it was candles, and…'

My voice was drowned out in a sea of cheers. 'Three cheers for the monkey!' cried the English-speaking people. '*Vive le singe!*' cried the others.

'Eh?' said Dad.

The crowd broke through the gates, moved me aside, and lifted Thimble onto their shoulders.

'This monkey,' said the red-faced woman, 'is a hero!'

'I don't understand,' said Mum.

'For years we have lived in fear of this family,' said the woman. 'Now we will be rid of them forever!'

'You've lived in fear of Serge and Colette?' asked Mum.

The woman looked blank. 'This is not the

house of Serge and Colette,' she said. 'This is the house of notorious criminals, the Viborgs!'

'Eh?' said Dad.

The woman pointed next door. '*That* is the house of Serge and Colette,' she said.

Mum looked at me. 'Whose job was it to remember the right number, Jams?' she asked.

'Er … how old are you, Mum?' I asked. Those with a long memory may realise how I'd messed up, but what did that matter now? Serge and Colette's house was in perfect order, and we were the toast of Blingville!

'And now,' said the red-faced woman, 'we shall take you all to town and buy you the biggest feast you can eat!'

The crowd cheered, but Dad suddenly

held his stomach. 'Actually,' he said, 'I feel a bit...'

Uh-oh. Was this the revenge of the sausages?

'BLE-U-RRRRRCH!' went Dad, and up came the dinner I'd lovingly cooked, in chunky soup form, all down his front. There was a gasp from the crowd, but Dad actually started laughing. 'This,' he burbled, 'is Mr Viborg's best suit!'

The crowd went wild. 'You are a funny man!' someone shouted.

Dad looked delighted. 'That's right! I am funny! You must read my books!'

Needless to say everyone was fascinated to hear about Dad's books and insisted he sent over a crate of them when we got back to Britain, so that they could make him as famous in France as he claimed to be back home. So I mentioned that I was also a writer, and they were even more interested in me, and lifted me up on their shoulders alongside my greatest pal. Someone found Dad some nice clean clothes, then Mum and Dad lined up on either side and together we set off down the street, heading for the feast of our lives. All our trials were forgotten, and once again life was a wonderful place, thanks to the one and only Thimble Monkey Superstar.

Praise for *Thimble Monkey Superstar*

'An absolutely hilarious story, deservedly shortlisted for the Lollies, Laugh Out Loud Book Awards. This is an imaginative tale,with sharp one liners and a truly batty adventure which is still making me giggle!'
Zoe James-Williams, South Wales Evening Post

'Madcap humour, corny one-liners and ludicrous situations abound in this light-hearted chapter book… The illustrations are suitably wild and wacky and the short, snappy text make this an accessible and fast-paced adventure.'
BookTrust

'It's very funny and the text positively bristles with jokes and snappy one-liners, the butt of most of them being Jams' hapless dad. Nicely divided into satisfying chapters and full of Martin Chatterton's wonderful bug-eyed illustrations, this is easy and addictive reading.' *Andrea Reece, Lovereading4kids*

'A charming and funny book. We really enjoyed the exploits of the mischievous and fiendishly clever monkey.'
Toppsta review

'This book is a must.'
Toppsta review

'A funny, delightful book.'
Boyd Clack

'It was really refreshing to have a main character with
a disability – doesn't happen very often. I think it' s a
great book for all children!'
Toppsta review

'Jams is awesome – he's smart, he's strong and he's
funny. We loved Thimble – my son has told me he
would love to have a pet monkey too!'
Toppsta review

'*Thimble Monkey Superstar* is hilarious ... this is
a truly engaging book, full of hilarious slapstick
episodes which invariably end with egg on Dad's face.'
Family Bookworms

THIMBLE MONKEY SUPERSTAR

by Jon Blake, illustrated by Martin Chatterton

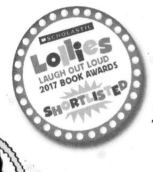

SHORTLISTED FOR THE
**LOLLIES LAUGH-OUT-LOUD
AWARDS 2017**

Selected for the
Summer Reading Challenge 2017 and
Toppsta Summer Reading Guide 2017

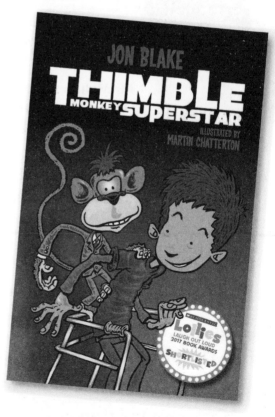

- **Firefly Press 2016**

- **£5.99**

- **ISBN:**
978-1-910080-34-4